A Little World For You

First Edition.
ISBN 978-0-9981569-0-3

Dedicated To

Aya, the most beautiful mom in the world

and

Dada, an amazing guitarist and rock star

Special Thanks
Grandma Seiko and Grandpa Koji
Grandma Mom and Grandpa Bob
Aunt Mimi
Aunt Sis
Aunt Tammy
Aunt Freddie
Aunt Sandy
Uncle Tom
Uncle Mas
Uncle David
Uncle Sam
Uncle Bill
Uncle Patrick
Kiyana, Matthew, and Ryan
Alana and Dave
Amelia and Ryan
Max and Megan
Marin
Caroline and Peter
Jack
Tessa and Gus
Samantha, for inspiring me to draw!
Miya and Mike
My Kenter Crew: Fosse, Rebecca, Dessery, Pauline and Portia
Michael Ware
Chelsea Treat
Pali Lacrosse Team
Sammy S
Cindy P, Claire S and Lilly W
Angel E
Gloria Castro
Krystle Scott
Luba and Wally
Mr. Vieira
Ms. Castro
Best Golf Coach Mr. Paleno
My Wonderful Art Teacher Ms. Villagran
Ryman Arts
In Memory of James

Counting Sheep

I've got sheep in my room

They escaped from my head

I was trying to fall asleep

Counting sheep

But instead

They are baaaaing and baaaaing

All over my room

Oh dear

I don't think I will be getting to bed

anytime soon

If I were able to

I would give you the world

So you could put it on your bedside table

And I'd place some stars in the sky to light up your world

And some boys and some girls

And I'd pour water in all the gaps

So they could swim, have fun and laugh

I'd hang some clouds above your world

And from time to time they'd make it rain

Oh, your world would be anything but plain!

On opposite sides

A sun

A moon

One for me

and one for you

your world would be filled with light

and all through the day and the night

everything would be alright

I would scatter music all around

A secret treasure to be found

And songs would flow throughout the land

Different styles, different bands

And in your world,

there would be so much love

As warm as a winter glove

If I were able to, I'd give you the world...

But you already have it

It is in your hands

The world is waiting

On everybody's bedside stand

I haven't got a house

With doors that open wide

I haven't got a home

With windows that show the sky

I live out in the garden

'cause I'm a garden gnome

so I call the whole front yard and stretching world

my home sweet home

Apple Pie

Apple pie

Me oh my

Criss crossed crust

Cinnamon spice

Everything nice

Just a little touch

Crispy dreams

On happy tongues

Warm aromas

On the run

Oven baked

Golden flaked

Like the California sun

Bird's Nest

Silly silly Cydney

Would not brush her hair

So much so

It turned into a bird's nest up there!

A family of finches moved in

With suitcases and worms

They built a lovely kitchen

And silly Cydney didn't even squirm

Next they built a chimney

And roasted marshmallows with glee

For silly Cydney's nest of hair

Had rent that was free

Chocolate Chip Cookie Dough

DON'T eat the cookies raw

That's what she said

But raw dough is my favorite

So I went on ahead

And I woke up this morning

Feeling awfully strange

I looked in the mirror

My have I changed!

My hair has turned into melted chocolate chips

My face is so doughy

And so are my lips

I squish when I walk

The dog follows me around

I can barely move my squashy feet

Off the ground

But on the plus side,

I taste great!

A Poem For You

Do you want to hear a poem?

Why, I wrote one just for you

It started with hello and talked about what you
do

I continued by comparing you to a fresh spring
flower

In the middle of an April rain shower

And it went on from there

I believed I mentioned the color of your eyes

And the softness of your hair

It spoke of how long I loved you

And how I'll continue to do so

It spoke of your tender words

And how you'll continue to grow

Do you want to hear the poem?

Well I do too

 This is the poem

that I wrote for you!

A lion talked to me mom

Look, right there!

What did he say?

Why, he loves my hair!

Boo the Bunny

Up and down

Up and down

the other bunnies hopped

but when Little Boo the Bunny

tried to hop

He'd always land with a PLOP!

So Little Bunny Boo

What did he do,

to jump up high?

He bought a big, bouncy trampoline

and now he hops to the clouds in the sky!

sticky

Pancakes pancakes

Stacked to the sky

Pancakes pancakes

Up a mile high

Sticky syrup

dripping

On my very

eyes

But that's

what happens

When you

stack

pancakes

Oh so high

best friends

a best friend is a hand to hold

a jacket-lender when you are cold

someone to laugh with

to live with

wild and free

and in this world

it's just my

best friend and me

Please, please?!

I'd clean up all his messes

and pour him water everyday

I'd pet his head

and teach him to follow what I say

I'd walk him every morning

you wouldn't have to do a thing!

think about it!

what joy a pet like him could bring

I'd pay for all his food

and even make him a bed

and if he can't use the bathtub

I'll wash him outside instead

He would always smell great

Why, I'll even brush his teeth

and read him a story

before we both fall asleep

C'mon it'll be great

you won't even have to pay

please please please

Can I get a pet dragon today?

Do you have any metal lying around?

Any doodads, trinkets, screws and pins to be found?

An engine, a fire, a big gas balloon?

Because I am building my very own rocket and I want to get to the moon soon!

Cheese

Stan from down the street

says the moon is made of cheese

and that's mostly all

that aliens ever eat

they grate it onto nachos

and make creamy mac and cheese

they swim in milk rivers

and eat as much as they please

they bake giant pizzas

and dance all around

because they've got the most cheese

in the universe,

that can be found!

Hungry!

I am stuffing my face with pizza

and crispy french fries

steamy mashed potato mountains

that reach up to the sky

grilled beef patties

sizzling hot dogs

pretzels salty and sweet

buttery corn, just popped

ooey gooey macaroni

a cheesy dish delight

a whole Thanksgiving dinner

roasted turkey

cooked just right

sandwiches stacked

with peanut butter

and jiggling jelly

all this yummy food

going into my belly

a huge stack of pancakes

stretched a mile high

because maybe if I eat as much as a

caterpillar

I'll become a butterfly!

Jim

My pet Jim doesn't do much
he just sits and stares
I drag him when we go on walks
and have to carry him up the stairs
he weighs an awful lot
and is really hard to move
he leaves dents in the ground
and always feels very smooth
I don't ever have to feed him
and he's quiet enough to come to school
he likes to sit out in the garden all day
or take a sinking swim in the pool
when I brought him to show and tell
I got quite a shock
Because my teacher said, "Why, that's no pet at all,
it's just a rock!"

Treasures

I have steered ships bigger than the eye can see

I have even sailed across the seven seas

I have found gold, rubies, and diamonds

buried deep

but all the riches

I have seen

I've never wanted to keep

because who needs shiny rocks

and a collection of things

when friendship and adventure

are the most valuable riches

anyone ever needs

Broccoli

You can't make me eat that vile stuff

that gross, green, mushy muck

that branched boiled broccoli

something that tastes so bad

can't possibly be good for me!

Don't put it one inch closer

Ahhh I'm not gonna chew it!

Hang on a second...

This broccoli stuff is pretty good

I just never knew it!

My pet giraffe Brunn

is a pretty cool guy

his long neck almost touches the stars

in the sky!

Brunn is like a brown spotted ladder

he works like a set of stairs

he lets me climb up his neck

and when we're out in town

we get odd stares

He can reach all the goodies

on the top shelf in the kitchen

He always grabs me the cookie jar

and from treetops, he rescues kittens!

So if you ever have a chance

to get a pet giraffe like Brunn

I really recommend it

You guys will have so much fun!

Bedtime

When I lay my head to sleep

on a comfy cotton pillow

my sheets

like sails in the wind

billow

and I am whisked away

to the island of dreams

but I am not scared

because my ferocious bear Teddy

protects me

Billy's Beans

Billy bought magic beans

from a man in a shop

he planted them into the dirt

and fed 'em water drops

he waited patiently

for those magic beans to grow

and with some love and light

the ground began to glow

out sprung a twig

with light green leaves

and soon after

grew a whole cherry tree

and gardening is still the greatest magic

Billy can barely believe!

Masterpiece

I have seen skies filled with fluffy clouds

that stretch like wisps of cotton candy

I have seen the ocean's changing tides

and daisies that make the world dandy

I have seen never-ending horizons

flowing waterfalls and rivers

I have seen snow and blue frozen lakes

a sight that gives me shivers

I am not sure how this beautiful world came to be

but I do know that it's the greatest work of art

I will ever see

Busy Bees

Buzz the Bee

sells jars of honey

down the winding road

he wraps them up in pretty paper

and then he is ready to go

the hungry bears

wait everyday

for the yummy snack

as Buzz the Bee

and his helper friends

deliver the honey as a pack

They give each bear a jar

of the gooey golden honey

and in return

the bears give Buzz money

then Buzz and his friends

buy big, beautiful flowers

so the cycle never ends

and they can make more honey for hours

Greedy Gary Goo
went to an ice-cream store
and kept asking the scooper
for more and more and more
chocolate chip and strawberry
give me
give me
all I see
cotton candy and lemon sorbet
C'mon, it's a really hot day!
minty milk and cookie dough
my, did that stack of ice cream grow!
so many scoops
slopping and sliding about
balancing and swaying
in and out
the stack teetered and tottered
leaned this way and that
it creaked and crackled
then fell with a SPLAT
and Greedy Gary Goo
finally understood why they say
"don't be greedy Gary,
 you only need one scoop a day!"

My Pet Time

Have you seen my pet Time?

Why, I've been looking all around town

But my pet Time, is nowhere to be found

You see, I lost him this morning

When I tried to check my email

But I got lost in the letters

And my pet Time decided to bail

I lost him again

Today at school

When I was supposed to be studying

But I was busy blowin' bubbles

Pretending to be cool

And every time I find him

He seems to leave again

Like a clockwise circle that keeps goin'

A never ending friend

Oh, there he is!

There is my pet time!

I better go catch him

Before I lose him again

Trying to make this sentence rhyme...

Pizza Pie

I have never seen anything more beautiful

Than a full pizza pie

Cheesy gooey goodness

That makes me want to fly

Pepperoni speckled like stars

Across a cheese cloud sky

Tomato sauce oceans

A universe you can buy

Palm tree swaying

Give me a high five

I'd like one from you

If I could reach up that high

Queen of Cats

Carmen says she is the Queen of Cats

Well they do follow her around

She says she has magic cat powers

And can understand all their sounds

She says that when she talks to them

They meow back, "All hail the Queen!"

Sometimes Carmen says she is a cat

And even dresses as one when it's not Halloween

Maybe Carmen is the Queen of Cats

But just yesterday

I saw her sneak a big fat fish into her pocket

So the cats would follow her away

I am a ruler of a kingdom

not far from here

where the water meets the shore

and worries disappear

I live in a castle

with flapping flags and a moat

I even own my very own boat

I built the castle myself

with shovels and sand

I am the ruler

of a sandcastle kingdom

and all the surrounding land

The Side Roads

There is traffic

all around us

All these cars are starting to surround us

But I know a magic trick

To get out of this rut very quick

Take the side roads my friend

You see, waiting with the herd is a dead end

Sure the other paths are not very clear

But they are better than the path here

And maybe they are a bit overgrown

But the more we see

The more we know

Are you scared we'll get lost?

Why there is no such thing!

See, with minds like mine and yours

There's so much we can bring

So let's be on our way

If everyone's taking the same path

That's where they'll stay

We don't have much time to lose

C'mon now

Choose!

Fireworks

Stars of different colors

Light up the dark sky

Paint it red and blue

Then disappear

Way up high

We sit on the damp grass ground

Watching all night

As colored stars burst above us

Bringing the world to life

Randy Abbot

always dreamed of being

somewhere that he was not

He'd want to go to the beach

but then he'd say it was too hot

He'd always think of the future

or of the past

as soon as he'd get where he was going

he'd want to leave, and fast

Randy Abbot

would climb up mountains

then change his mind

He'd walk all the way to the forest

but then say it was a waste of time

Randy Abbot

spent all his life

looking for the next place

so he never truly enjoyed

any of the wonders

right in front of his face

there he goes   again!

when Sam first played the drums

she was awful

just bad

but she played every day

'cause it was the best hobby she had

and so the seasons passed

and Sam kept playing on

she banged those drums every morning

and made her own unique song

and the neighbors would holler

say she's no good

but Sam kept on practicing

like a musician should

Sam kept on playing

BOOM, BADOOM, CRASH!

she hit those symbols

and at last...

she became magnificent!

she was just great

she had rhythm and style

so people would wait

for hours and hours

to hear her play

at last crowds and crowds (even her neighbors) would cheer

HURRAY!

Tooth Fairy

Yesterday I lost a tooth

it popped straight out

after I spent the whole morning

wiggling it all about

so I put it under my pillow

I tucked it in with care

I thought it grew legs and feet

Because the next morning, it wasn't there!

but in its little spot I saw

a note just for me

with sparkly glitter and a coin

from the magical tooth fairy!

* How to Make the Most Delicious Hamburger Ever! *

The Chef says to his son,

"First, goes the bun

then the cheese

next the lettuce

and some tomatoes please

now barbecued beef

nice and fresh

keep going

don't forget the rest!"

the son says,

"let's make a burger

that can stretch all the way to the moon!

we'll add macaroni

pepperoni

and a giant mushroom

oh! let's add

hot sausages

vanilla donuts

a custard cheese pie

two oranges

bouncy birthday cake

pb & j on rye"

the Chef says, "and the last step,

the very top bun!"

"wow!" said the son,

"who knew that making a burger

could be so much fun!"

Did you know that shoes can fly?

Well neither did I

Until I heard the tale...

Flying shoes do as they please

They do not like smelly feet

or being worn on knees

They do not like hot pavement

or stepping in goo

and sticky icky bubble gum

certainly will not do!

so flying shoes do as they please

they flap their laces

above the trees

but some get stuck along the way

Don't believe me? Look up at a telephone wire today!

Bob and his Cat Cap

Bob was going to a ball game

but he couldn't find a hat

so he placed upon his head

his very furry cat

it did not block the sun

it did not block the wind

but his cat did catch a flying foul ball

and for Bob,

that was definitely a win!

Procrastination

I'd rather watch paint dry

and see the grass grow

dust off all the knick knacks

lined up in a row

I'd rather do the dirty dishes

and scrub the bubbling bathtub

I'd rather give the goldfish kisses

and the scratching cat a hug

I'd rather tidy up my messy room

or clean filthy floors with a broken broom

but please, oh please

don't make me do my homework soon!

fly bird

fly bird

up to the sky

if I could fly like you

my, would I fly

I would soar over the world

and see this city from a bird's eye

fly bird

fly bird

way up high

It's Christmas in California

and I haven't seen a single snowflake

but it's a snowman

I really want to make

so I made a sandman instead

'cause sand is all we got

and he is way cooler than a snowman

'cause he doesn't melt when it gets hot

Nothing to Wear

Hello, hello, is anyone there?

I have absolutely nothing to wear!

I have searched every room of my house

And still don't have a wearable blouse

I have sailed the seven seas

In search of some pants for me

But all I seem to see

Is an endless stretch of empty

What, what is that you say?

Complain another day?

No, no that cannot be

No I do not have piles of clothes behind me

Well...

I do you see

But those clothes are not pleasing to me!

you light up my life

like nothing has before

you are the best lamp

anyone could ever ask for

Good Night!